For Francesca

BEACH LANE BOOKS • An imprint of Simon & Schuster Children's Publishing Division • 1230 Avenue of the Americas. New York. New York 10020 • Copyright © 2018 by Alison Lester • First published in Australia in 2018 by Allen & Unwin • All rights reserved. including the right of reproduction in whole or in part in any form. • BEACH LANE BOOKS is a trademark of Simon & Schuster. Inc. • For information about special discounts for bulk purchases. please contact Simon & Schuster Special Sales at 1-866-506-1949 or business@simonandschuster.com. • The Simon & Schuster Speakers Bureau can bring authors to your live event. For more information or to book an event. contact the Simon & Schuster Speakers Bureau at 1-866-248-3049 or visit our website at www.simonspeakers.com. • Book design by Lauren Rille • The text for this book was set in Plumbsky. • Manufactured in China • 0319 SCP • First Edition • 10 9 8 7 6 5 4 3 2 1 • Library of Congress Cataloging-in-Publication Data • Names: Lester. Alison. author. illustrator. • Title: Noni the pony rescues a joey / Alison Lester. • Description: First edition. | New York : Beach Lane Books. [2019] | Originally published in Australia by Allen & Unwin in 2018. | Summary: Noni and her friends help a lost wallaby joey find his family. • Identifiers: LCCN 2018039908 | ISBN 9781534443709 (hardcover : alk. paper) | ISBN 9781534443716 (eBook) • Subjects: | CYAC: Stories in rhyme. | Ponies-Fiction. | Wallabies-Fiction. | Lost children-Fiction. • Classification: LCC PZ8.3.L54935 Nt 2019 | DDC [E]-dc23 LC record available at https://lccn.loc.gov/2018039908

Alison Lester

noni the pony
rescues a joey

BEACH LANE BOOKS   New York   London   Toronto   Sydney   New Delhi

Noni the Pony lives near the sea.
She's friendly and frisky and loves running free.

With Coco and Dave she heads out for the day
to roam in the hills behind Waratah Bay.

The friends wander down a leafy green trail,
where they meet someone small with a very long tail.

It's a wallaby joey, all on his own,
who says in a soft voice, "I want to go home."

"I was chasing a gum leaf the north wind had tossed, and when I stopped hopping, I found myself lost."

"Come with us, then," says Noni. "We'll ask on our way.
Your wallaby mob can't be too far away."

They call to Koala, high in a tree.
But she says, "I'm sleeping. Please don't bother me."

"Wallabies?" says Wombat. "Haven't seen them around.
I've been in my burrow, deep underground."

Shy Platypus has nothing to say.
She dives in the creek and splashes away.

And Emu, who's guarding his chicks in the grass,
says, "Sorry, I haven't seen anyone pass."

Echidna's been digging, with no time for peeping,
and Possum, Goanna, and Quoll are all sleeping.

No one has spotted the wallaby mob,
and Joey's small sniffle becomes a big sob.

"Don't cry," says Noni. "Give us a smile.
Come back to our place and stay for a while."

When they get back to their home by the bay,
the last rays of sunlight have faded away.

But who do they see in the twilight's dim glow?
The wallaby family, looking for Joe!

The ladies next door moo a beautiful tune.
And they all hop and bop by the light of the moon.

"Bye-bye, little Joe...

see you soon!"